I'm *Geronimo Stilton*'s sister. As I'm sure you know from my brother's bestselling novels, I'm a special correspondent for *The Rodent's Gazette*, Mouse Island's most famous newspaper. Unlike my 'fraidy mouse brother, I absolutely adore traveling, having adventures, and meeting rodents from all around the world!

The adventure I want to tell you about begins at Mouseford Academy, the school I went to when I was a young mouseling. I had such a great experience there as a student that I came back to teach a journalism class.

When I returned as a grown mouse, I met five really special students: Colette, Nicky, Pamela, Paulina, and Violet. You could hardly imagine five more different mouselings, but they became great friends right away. And they liked me so much that they decided to name their group after me: the Thea Sisters! I was so touched by that, I decided to write about their adventures. So turn the page to read a fabumouse adventure about the

THEA SISTERS!

Nicky

Name: Nicky
Nickname: Nic
Home: Australia
Secret ambition: Wants to be an ecologist.
Loves: Open spaces and nature.
Strengths: She is always in a good mood, as long as she's outdoors!
Weaknesses: She can't sit still!
Secret: Nicky is claustrophobic—she can't stand being in small, tight places.

Nicky

COLETTE

Name: Colette

Nickname: It's Colette, please. (She can't stand nicknames.)

Home: France

Secret ambition: Colette is very particular about her appearance. She wants to be a fashion writer.

Loves: The color pink.

Strengths: She's energetic and full of great ideas.

Weaknesses: She's always late!

Secret: To relax, there's nothing Colette likes more than a manicure and pedicure.

Colette

VIOLET

Name: Violet
Nickname: Vi
Home: China
Secret ambition: Wants to become a great violinist.
Loves: Books! She is a real intellectual, just like my
brother, Geronimo.
Strengths: She's detail-oriented and always open to
new things.
Weaknesses: She is a bit sensitive and can't stand
being teased. And if she doesn't get enough sleep,
she can be a real grouch!
Secret: She likes to unwind by listening
to classical music and drinking green tea.

Violet

Name: Paulina
Nickname: Polly
Home: Peru
Secret ambition: Wants to be a scientist.
Loves: Traveling and meeting people from all over the world. She is also very close to her sister, Maria.
Strengths: Loves helping other rodents.
Weaknesses: She's shy and can be a bit clumsy.
Secret: She is a computer genius!

PAULINA

PAULINA

Name: Pamela
Nickname: Pam
Home: Tanzania
Secret ambition: Wants to become a sports journalist or a car mechanic.
Loves: Pizza, pizza, and more pizza! She'd eat pizza for breakfast if she could.
Strengths: She is a peacemaker. She can't stand arguments.
Weaknesses: She is very impulsive.
Secret: Give her a screwdriver and any mechanical problem will be solved!

Pamela

Geronimo Stilton

Thea Stilton
AND THE LEGEND
OF THE FIRE FLOWERS

Scholastic Inc.

ISBN 978-0-545-48188-5

Based on an original idea by Elisabetta Dami.

www.geronimostilton.com

Published by Scholastic Inc., 557 Broadway, New York, NY 10012.
SCHOLASTIC and associated logos are trademarks and/or registered trademarks of Scholastic Inc.

Stilton is the name of a famous English cheese. It is a registered trademark of the Stilton Cheese Makers' Association. For more information, go to www.stiltoncheese.com.

Text by Thea Stilton
Original title *La leggenda dei fiori di fuoco*
Cover by Arianna Rea (pencils), Yoko Ippolitoni (inks), and Ketty Formaggio (color)
Illustrations by Sabrina Ariganello, Michela Frare, Daniela Geremia, Cristina Giorgilli, Gaetano Petrigno, Arianna Rea, Raffaella Seccia, and Roberta Tedeschi
Color by Cinzia Antonielli, Giorgia Arena, Alessandra Bracaglia, Laura Brancati, and Edwyn Nori
Graphics by Paola Cantoni with Marta Lorini

Special thanks to Beth Dunfey
Translated by Emily Clement
Interior design by Kay Petronio

12 11 10 9 8 7 6 5 4   14 15 16 17 18/0

Printed in the U.S.A.   40
First printing, June 2013

THEA SISTERS NOW MORE THAN EVER!

Just a few months ago, I would never have dreamed that my friends the **THEA SISTERS** would *surpass* me as investigative journalists. But it's happened, and I am *prouder* than a porcupine!

Who are the Thea Sisters? Why, they are my former students at **MOUSEFORD ACADEMY.**

You see, a little while back, I was invited to teach a class in adventure journalism at my old school. Colette, Nicky, PAMELA, PAULINA, and **Violet** — the Thea Sisters — were in my class. Without a doubt, they are the five most **brilliant** mouselets I've ever met.

In fact, they are such good detectives that they've solved almost as many **mysteries** as my old friend Hercule Poirat!

But I'm putting the **CHEESE** before the cracker. Let me slow down and begin at the *beginning*.

A few days ago, my brother, *Geronimo*, called me into his office at *The Rodent's Gazette*. (He is the publisher, and I am a special correspondent.) As soon as I scampered in, he pawed me a hot-off-the-press copy of the newspaper.

"Congratulations, sis! Those mouselets of yours have gotten a **REAL SCOOP**!"

I took the newspaper and immediately spotted a photo of my young friends on the front page.

"The Thea Sisters!" I exclaimed in surprise. Geronimo nodded in satisfaction.

I began to read out loud: "'Five Mouseford Academy **students** perform heroic rescue atop **Hawaii's** biggest **Volcano**'!"

"You did a fabumouse job training those mouselets. Great work!" my brother said.

"What do you say to a trip to **WHALE ISLAND**? I want your pals to give you an exclusive interview so we can publish a special edition of *The Rodent's Gazette*."

He didn't have to ask twice. I grabbed the **ferry** ticket he'd bought me, slapped a kiss on his snout, and scurried home to pack my **bags**.

When the ferry pulled into port, Colette, Nicky, Pamela, Paulina, and Violet were standing on the pier, waving eagerly. They couldn't wait to tell me about the **INCREDIBLE** adventure that had splashed their snouts across **NEWSPAPERS** all over the world!

We hugged and hurried up to the school. Violet fixed us a pot of PIPING-HOT tea, and the mouselets began to tell me their tale, starting with the moment they arrived in **Hawaii**. . . .

A BREATHTAKING VIEW

"Sizzling spark plugs, mouselets! Check it out. Now *that's* what I call a BREATHTAKING view!" Pam cried.

The Thea Sisters' plane was about to land at Hilo International Airport. Pam's EYES were glued to the window, and over and over she squeaked, "**Fabumouse!**"

After Pam's zillionth exclamation, Colette looked up from her pawnail polish. "So, Pam, are you are happy to be in Hawaii or not?" She grinned as her friend spluttered, "Uh, yeah!"

Pam finally **peeled** herself away from the window, leaving a

Kaulakahi Channel

Kauai

HANALEI

KAPAA

PU'UWAI KEKAHA LIHUE

Kauai Channel

Oahu

LAIE

WAIALUA HALEIWA

WAHIAWA KAILUA

Niihau

HONOLULU

PACIFIC OCEAN

Hawaii is an archipelago of many volcanic islands that emerged millions of years ago in the middle of the Pacific Ocean. The main islands include Hawaii (also known as the Big Island) and seven other, smaller islands. The three biggest cities are Hilo (on the island of Hawaii), Honolulu, and Kailua (on the island of Oahu).

The Hawaiian islands are famous for their beautiful beaches, lush forests, volcanic deserts, and spectacular views.

THE HAWAIIAN ISLANDS

Country: United States of America
Capital: Honolulu (on the island of Oahu)
Languages: English and Hawaiian
Currency: United States Dollars (USD)

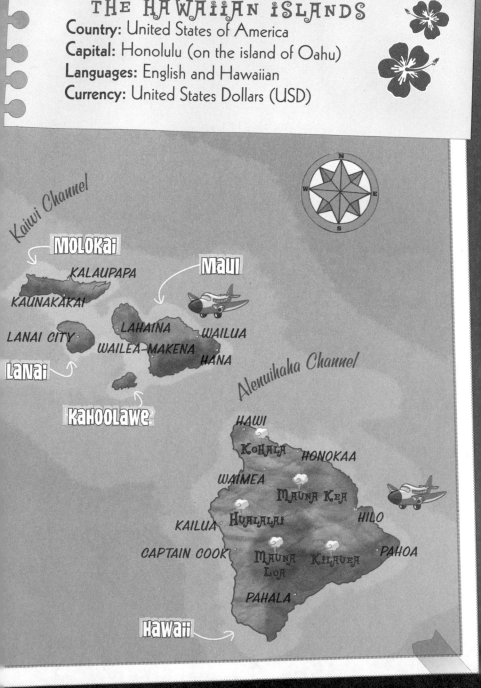

Kaiwi Channel

MOLOKAI

KALAUPAPA

KAUNAKAKAI

MAUI

LANAI CITY

LAHAINA

WAILUA

WAILEA-MAKENA

Lanai

HANA

Kahoolawe

Alenuihaha Channel

HAWI

KOHALA

HONOKAA

WAIMEA

MAUNA KEA

KAILUA

HUALALAI

HILO

CAPTAIN COOK

MAUNA LOA

KILAUEA

PAHOA

PAHALA

Hawaii

smudgy snout print behind. "Why, did I already mention it?"

"At least twenty-five times!" said Paulina, winking. Then, when she saw that her friend was sensitive about being **teased**, she hugged her. "Snout up, Pam! You know we love how jolly you are. You are the official cheerleader of the Thea Sisters!"

"Everyone needs to look out the window **immediately**!" exclaimed Violet suddenly from

the seat behind them. "We're **Flying over** Hawaii's volcanoes. There are five of them, and they are unbelievable!"

Pam and Paulina **TURNED** around. Violet was pointing out the mouth of each volcano.

"See, what did I tell you mouselings? This place is amazing!" commented Pam. "Even Violet says so, and she's never wrong!"

Colette, Nicky, Paulina, and Violet *burst out laughing*.

A moment later, the scratchy squeak of the pilot distracted them from the **view**. The plane was coming in for a landing. As soon as it touched ground, the passengers began gathering their carry-on bags.

"Come on, mouselets, let's shake a tail!" urged Colette, stowing her pawnail polish inside her cosmetics case, where she had at least ten different SHADES OF PINK.

"It's time to go, go, go! The HULA competition awaits!" She looked around to make sure she had everything. That's when she noticed another group of mouselets waiting to get off the plane. Colette sighed. It was the RUBY CREW!

LEI MEANS HELLO!

As the **THEA SISTERS** scrambled off the plane, they noticed the Ruby Crew — Ruby, Alicia, Connie, and Zoe — eyeing them. Ruby and her three friends also attended **MOUSEFORD ACADEMY**, but they didn't seem to like the Thea Sisters very much. In fact, they tended to be pretty SNOBBY toward most of the other students at Mouseford.

"Well, I'm less psyched about participating in the HULA championship now that I've seen some of the **competition**," Pam grumbled.

"YEAH," sighed Colette. "Talk about bad luck! I didn't realize there was more than one team here representing **MOUSEFORD**.

Sometimes I feel like the Ruby Crew are bobcats stalking their prey — us!"

Violet **SHRUGGED** serenely. "Rise above, sisters. We're on vacation! Let's just **relax** and enjoy it. As Grandpa Chen used to say, 'To every rodent her own cheese puff!'"

The **mouselets** scurried into the airport and were overcome by a *wave* of energy: The atrium was filled with students from all over the world! Ukelele music *echoed* through the airport. There was a group of Hawaiian mice **dancing** the hula to welcome everyone who had just landed.

"**CRUSTY CARBURETORS**, this is marvemouse!" cried Pam.

Nicky nodded enthusiastically. "I LOVE this place already, and we haven't even set paw outside the airport!"

At that moment, a group of dancers approached the THEA SISTERS and placed some very colorful, flowery wreaths around their necks.

"Lei!" said one dancer, giving Pam a gorgeous WREATH.

"Hey, thanks! So, what does *lei* mean?" asked Pam, admiring her new neckwear.

The dancer **smiled**. "In our language, a lei is a wreath of *flowers*. It's our way of saying **hello**. Welcome to Hawaii!"

HULA

Hula is a traditional Hawaiian dance known for its graceful, undulating movements. It has been called "the heartbeat of the Hawaiian people." Hula is a form of storytelling, and it is often accompanied by *mele*, a chant or song. The older style of *hula*, known as *kahiko*, is accompanied by traditional musical instruments like drums, bamboo canes, and gourds filled with seeds.

The more modern strain, *hula'auana*, is performed with Western instruments like the guitar and the ukulele.

Hula is the embodiment of many important Hawaiian cultural traditions — poetry, religion, history, martial arts, and much more. Competing cultures have threatened hula in the past. But today, after a cultural revival during the 1970s, hula is stronger than ever.

ATTIRE

Originally, women wore short skirts and men wore loincloths to dance the hula. Today, they wear fabric skirts whose colors represent the different schools of hula. Dancers also wear bracelets and anklets made of shells or whale teeth. Their heads and necks are decorated with flowers.

Hula is known all over the world, and there are dozens of festivals held each year in Hawaii. Hilo's Merrie Monarch Festival is the world's most prestigious hula competition. The event is dedicated to the memory of an ancient ruler of Hawaii, King David Kalākaua.

THE WHITE DOG

The **mouselets** and the other contestants left the Hilo airport together. The Thea Sisters were already **BONDING** with the other competitors — everyone except for the Ruby Crew, that is. Ruby and her friends trailed after the rest of the rodents. They only seemed interested in *chatting* with one another.

As they were all boarding the **bus** that would take them to the resort,* a squeak rang out: "Look! A WHITE DOG!"

Colette, Nicky, Pamela, Paulina, and Violet turned around. A Hawaiian **mouselet** was pointing at something in the distance. She seemed very worried.

Tails trembling, her friends surrounded

---

*A resort is a fancy hotel that offers services like swimming pools, a spa, meeting rooms, and even concerts.

CLUE!

her. They all shared the same **fearful** expression.

The Thea Sisters followed their **gaze** and saw a white dog passing about twenty feet away.

Colette, Nicky, Pam, Paulina, and Violet exchanged puzzled looks: What was so **SCARY** about a white dog?

"Let's do a little research when we get to the hotel," Violet whispered to Paulina, who nodded.

After a short **DRIVE**, the bus stopped in front of a *flashy* new building. The sign outside read FIRE FLOWERS RESORT. It looked very *exclusive*!

"Holey cheese!" cried Pamela as she scrambled off the bus. "What a fancy-schmancy hotel! The owners must have

Why were the local mouselets so upset by the sight of an ordinary white dog?

MONEY to burn. . . ."

"You said it, sis!" chirped Colette, her eyes sparkling. "I'll bet there's a **spa** inside!"

Paulina and Nicky looked at her in confusion. "A *what*?"

"A spa is a **beauty** treatment center," Colette explained. "A place where they help you relax with massages, snout masks, **compresses**, saunas —"

"We get it, Colette," interrupted Pam. "It's your ultimate fantasy made reality!"

Nicky and Paulina **BURST** into giggles.

SPA

The word *spa* comes from the town of Spa in Belgium, where people used to visit for the healing properties of its mineral springs. Today the term is used to refer to centers that offer restorative hot baths, body well-being services, and beauty treatments.

"It sounds wonderful, Colette," said Violet gently. "But I don't know if there will be **TIME** for beauty treatments. We're here to represent Mouseford Academy in the **HULA** championship. We've got to stay focused on our performance tomorrow!"

A **HIGH-PITCHED** squeak interrupted her. "You said it, **SWEET CHEESE**! I'll bet you a pound of fresh Swiss that Mouseford will **win** the hula competition!"

RUBY'S CHALLENGE

It was Ruby squeaking. She, Connie, Zoe, and Alicia sashayed past the Thea Sisters.

"That's right, Ruby!" added Zoe. "But let me clear something up: Since the RUBY CREW is also here to represent Mouseford, the academy's got this competition in the palms of our paws. I can't imagine what a BAD IMPRESSION Mouseford would make if it were just the Thea Sisters representing our school!"

Pam was furious. "How dare you?! Just wait. We'll show you, you . . ."

Violet put a paw on her back to **calm** her down.

"Let it go, Pam! It's not worth getting upset about. At the end of the championship, the results will squeak for themselves!"

Ruby stuck her snout in the **air** and said, "I guess we'll see, won't we?" Then she shook her **FIERY** red fur and strode away, with her friends trailing after her.

That was when something **bizarre** happened: The mysterious WHITE DOG appeared again!

While everyone was entering the resort, an **old** mouse leaning on a wooden cane approached the group. He **LOOKED** very upset.

"Get out of here!" he shouted.

Everyone looked at him **apprehensively**. No one had any idea who this rodent was or why he was yelling at them.

"You must **LEAVE** immediately!" he

insisted. "Leave this hotel before Mauna Loa **ERUPTS**!"

The Thea Sisters exchanged **ALARMED** glances. They were about to ask the old gentlemouse for an explanation when Ruby butted in **IMPATIENTLY**. "Just ignore him. Obviously he doesn't know what he's talking about. Everything is so new here, there certainly can't be any **DANGER**!"

The other mice whispered a bit, but they reassured one another and agreed to ignore him.

"Come on, everyone," Ruby continued. "Let's relax and enjoy this *classy* hotel!"

At that moment, two **POLICE** officers came and grabbed the old gentlemouse.

"Come on, move along," the first officer

ordered him, dragging him away. "How many times have we told you not to scare the guests with your ridiculous stories?"

"Don't mind him," the other officer told the contestants. "He's CRAZIER than a cat chasing his own tail!"

Violet observed the two officers carefully. They

were dressed in official-looking uniforms, but they didn't **LOOK** like any policemice she'd ever seen.

The two officers nodded at a **mysterious mouse** standing at the entrance to the resort. He nodded back at them.

While the officers pulled the old gentlemouse away, he pointed his paw at the Thea Sisters, who were the only ones left **LOOKING AT HIM**. They **TURNED** to see what he was indicating and finally noticed the view. Looming over the resort was an enormouse **MOUNTAIN**: the Mauna Loa volcano!

CLUE!

 How strange! An elderly gentlemouse warned everyone to leave the resort, and two suspicious policemice dragged him away. Why? And who was that mysterious mouse watching over everything?

MAUNA LOA

Mauna Loa is the world's largest volcano. At its peak, it is 13,677 feet above sea level. Mauna Loa means "long mountain," and that is a good description of this volcano — it takes up half the area of the island of Hawaii, with a dome 75 miles long and 64 miles wide.

Mauna Loa has been an active volcano for over 100,000 years! It has erupted 33 times since its first documented explosion in 1843. The last eruption was in 1984.

WELCOME TO THE FIRE FLOWERS RESORT!

The Thea Sisters got settled in their room, which was more like a **deluxe** suite!

There were five canopy beds, each draped with a white curtain; an enormouse **hot tub** in the middle of the room; and a wall of windows that looked onto a pool of crystal CLEAR water. Mauna Loa stood imposingly in the background. What an **awe-inspiring** view!

The five mouselets lingered by the windows for a while, admiring the landscape. After a few moments, Colette broke the silence with an *excited* yelp: "Moldy Brie, there's a hooottt tuuuubbb!"

A hot tub!

Nicky, Pam, Paulina, and Violet laughed. Colette could be a little overly *enthusiastic*!

After unpacking their bags, the mouselets got ready to attend the **welcome party** downstairs. When they entered the banquet room, they immediately caught their **breath**: It had a magnificent terrace with an amazing view of Hilo Bay, which was **lit** up all the way out to *sea*.

"This place is swankier than soft cheese!"

commented Paulina, **IMPRESSED**.

The terrace was packed with young mice. Nicky noticed a **RatLet** gazing at her. She turned red and looked away, embarrassed. The Ruby Crew was there, too, dressed in their *fanciest* duds.

After a few moments, a mouse scurried onto a small platform at the end of the terrace and picked up a **MICROPHONE**. "Hello, everyone!" he exclaimed. "Welcome to the hula championship!"

"Isn't that the same rodent who **knew** the two police officers this afternoon?" whispered Violet. Her friends nodded in agreement.

"My name is Sammy Sharkfur, and I am the owner of this *marvemouse* resort!" the mouse continued PLeasantLy.

"*One* of the owners, that is," said another

mouse, SMILING, as he joined Sammy onstage. "Or are we not partners?"

Sharkfur turned **redder** than a tomato. "Oh, er, yes, yes, of course! I didn't mean to imply . . ." Turning back to the audience, he said: "It is with great pleasure that I introduce to you EKANA KAHANAMOKU, my

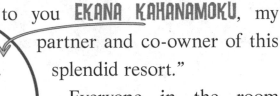

partner and co-owner of this splendid resort."

Everyone in the room applauded.

"Sharkfur doesn't seem too enthusiastic about having a partner, does he?" Paulina whispered.

"You can squeak that AGAIN," agreed Nicky.

While Ekana told everyone about the hula competition, Sharkfur climbed down from the platform and headed for a scraggy rodent with a pair of glasses perched on his snout. The rodent was holding a folder filled with papers under his paw. The two immediately began **SQUEAKING** nonstop.

Paulina shook her snout **SUSPICIOUSLY**. "I don't know about you, but there's something about Sammy Sharkfur that **rubs** my fur the wrong way. . . ."

As the Thea Sisters were **TALKING**, Sharkfur and the strange mouse slipped out of the room.

EKANA KAHANAMOKU

Ekana soon concluded his remarks. He climbed off the **platform** and began **CHATTING** with the guests. The Thea Sisters decided to go introduce themselves.

"**Hi!**" said Colette. "My name is Colette, and these are my friends Violet, Paulina, Nicky, and Pamela. We are here representing **MOUSEFORD ACADEMY.**"

"Welcome to *Hawaii*!" Ekana replied. "I hope you **enjoy** your stay, and most of all that you like our resort!"

"Are you kidding?!" responded Colette. "This place is just fabumouse!

Especially that HOT TUB in our room . . ."

Nicky jokingly put her paw over Colette's mouth, and Ekana laughed. "Well, I'm thrilled to meet such a BIG fan! We paid through the snout to get this hotel just right."

"Tell us a little about how the resort got started," Paulina jumped in. "Its location is amazing — right near MAUNA LOA. But isn't it dangerous?"

Ekana smiled calmly. "Absolutely not. The volcano has been dormant for years, and the island's observatory SURVEYED the land before we began construction on the resort. There is no danger at all!" Then he continued PROUDLY, "The land the hotel is built on has belonged to my family for generations. When Sammy arrived here, he asked me to be partners. We used my property to **BUILD** the resort."

Suddenly, Ekana's cell phone *rang*, and he excused himself.

The Thea Sisters exchanged glances. They had all noted the same thing: Sammy Sharkfur was the one who'd wanted to get into business with Ekana! **INTERESTING . . .**

Before returning to their room, the mouselets went onto the terrace, where some Hawaiian students were playing the **ukulele** under the gorgeous **NIGHT** sky.

"Isn't this place fantastic?" Paulina sighed dreamily. "It's more **MAGICAL** than Mouseyland!"

AN URGENT CALL FROM WHALE ISLAND!

The Thea Sisters wanted to get some **rest** before the competition began. They were heading **back** to their room when they ran into Ruby, Alicia, Zoe, and Connie in the corridor.

"You mouselings look a little ***tired***," observed Ruby, pretending to **worry**. "You better get some shut-eye, sleepysnouts! Otherwise your performance tomorrow will be even **WORSE** than usual! Ha ha ha!"

Before the Thea Sisters could respond, Ruby and her friends turned tail and DISAPPEARED into their room.

Then Paulina's MousePhone rang. She *quickly* answered it. To her surprise, it was Professor Van Kraken, their science teacher at Mouseford Academy.

The **mouselets** hurried into their room, and Paulina put the call on squeakerphone. "I'm so glad that I reached you!" began the professor. "I'm calling because there is an **EMERGENCY**, and only you can help me."

38

"You need us?!" exclaimed Pam, dumbfounded. "But, Professor, we are in Hawaii!"

"**Exactly!**" responded the professor. "That's why I'm asking for your **HELP**!"

Professor Van Kraken

"Sure, Professor," Pam said. "We are at your service. What's up?"

"I've been working with an international team of scientists, **monitoring** volcanoes around the world using the MOST MODERN research technology," explained the professor. "In the last few hours, we've collected some disturbing data about one of the volcanoes. An **ERUPTION** is close at paw. I'm squeaking about Mauna Loa!"

The mouselets jumped.

"But that's the **VOLCANO** right next to our resort!" exclaimed Nicky as the others **turned** to look out the window.

Professor Van Kraken **SENT** them a graph showing the data, and the mouselets gathered around to look at it. It was so **QUIET**, you could hear a cheese slice drop.

"This data shows that Mauna Loa will **ERUPT** within the next two days!" the professor cried in **ALARM**.

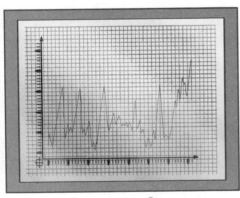

Paulina studied the chart carefully. "But just this evening, we talked to one of the two owners of the resort, and he assured us that Mauna Loa has been **dormant** for years. According to him, there are no **RISKS** of any kind. . . ."

"That worries me," said the professor. "I contacted **scientists** from the research

observatory on Mauna Loa, but they say they haven't seen any **WARNING** signs. That's impossible — the equipment our team placed there is the most recent technology and **can't be wrong**. There's something going on that I don't understand. . . ."

"You're right, that is really **strange**!" agreed Violet.

"A little *too* strange," said Professor Van Kraken. "But what's even stranger is that the local authorities let the resort be **BUILT** in that location. It is **TOO CLOSE** to the volcano!"

"Will we be **safe** if we stay here tonight?" asked Colette anxiously.

"Yes, I think so," said the professor. "Keep your phone with you at all times. I'll *call* you immediately if there is any sign of imminent **DANGER**."

"Of course!" said Paulina.

The professor was silent for a moment. "Mouselets, I absolutely do not mean to **scare you**, but I'm asking you to take advantage of where you are to **investigate** and, if necessary, intervene. Your resort could be *wiped out* by the eruption!"

LET'S REVIEW THE SITUATION:

- The Fire Flowers Resort is extremely close to the famous volcano Mauna Loa.
- Ekana Kahanamoku, one of the resort's owners, assured the Thea Sisters that Mauna Loa is a dormant volcano, and isn't dangerous. He says that the research observatory provided him with data assuring its safety before they began building the hotel.
- According to the data gathered by Professor Van Kraken, Mauna Loa is anything but dormant: It could erupt any minute!
- The scientists from the research observatory insist that there is no danger.
- How is it possible that Professor Van Kraken's team and the scientists from the research observatory have collected such different data?

THE COMPETITION BEGINS!

The next morning, Violet picked up the program for the competition and read it out loud.

❊ DAY ONE

MORNING   Group competition: traditional choreography
AFTERNOON   Free time

❊ DAY TWO

MORNING   Solo competition: traditional choreography
                Solo competition: modern choreography
                Group competition: modern choreography

AFTERNOON   Free time

❊ DAY THREE

MORNING   Semifinals and finals for groups and individuals
AFTERNOON   Awards ceremony

❊ DAY FOUR
ALOHA PARTY

The Thea Sisters were awake **early** — they wanted to get a head start on the first day of the competition. All five mouselets were feeling a little **nervous** as they pulled out the costumes Colette had designed for them.

"What do you think of the phone call last night?" asked Violet.

Paulina *sighed*. "I don't know. But one thing's for sure: Professor Van Kraken is very **SERIOUS** about his science. I'd be shocked if he made such a **BIG** mistake!"

"But if he's right, that would mean that the resort is in grave **DANGER**! And that Ekana lied to us," Nicky put in.

"What if he was just too trusting?" Pamela asked thoughtfully. "He doesn't seem like the type of mouse who would put anyone in danger on purpose. . . ." She zipped up her skirt and *twirled* around. "Wow, Colette,

these costumes are a dream! You really have a passion for fashion."

Colette giggled and waved her paw at Pam dismissively. But her friends knew she was beaming with **pride**.

"Let's try to concentrate on the HULA competition for now," said Violet as they headed out. "Maybe we can INVESTIGATE during our **free** time this afternoon."

The mouselets scurried toward the hotel's

main lobby, which was already **swarming** with young rodents from around the world. It looked like a field of colorful **flowers**! Everyone was wearing Hawaiian costumes designed specifically for the occasion.

The contestants boarded a **bus** and headed toward Hilo's Edith Kanaka'ole Stadium. When they arrived, musicians were already positioned around the stage, **READY** to play. The bleachers were packed and buzzing with excitement.

The local team, a group of mouselets from **HILO**, approached the Thea Sisters and introduced themselves.

"Hi!" one of them said. "My name is Apikalia, and these are my teammates. We wanted to compliment you on your costumes: They are really **divine**!"

Colette **lit up**. "Thanks so much!"

Ruby, who was °BSERVING the scene from afar, **ELBOWED** Alicia. "I told you that our costumes weren't glitzy enough! We let those Goody Two-paws beat us again. And it's all your fault!" She let out a big **sigh** and flounced away.

Alicia **looked** down in the snout. She never knew what to do when Ruby picked on her.

Just then, the judges ANNOUNCED the beginning of the competition. Then they called the Ruby Crew up to the stage. They would be the FiRST to perform.

THIS IS HULA!

The Ruby Crew's *choreography* was solid, if not superb. Alicia stumbled over a few steps, earning a **scathing** look from Ruby.

Next, the team from Maui was called up: Their performance was graceful and **energetic**. Nicky recognized the ratling that she had noticed the evening before. He was an agile and *elegant* dancer.

Then Apikalia's **GROUP** was called: The

movements of their paws and hips were in **perfect** sync, and the mouselets were as **supple** as **waves** on the ocean. They maintained perfect balance as they put in a fluid and **harmonious** performance. Now, *this* was hula! The mouselets were very impressed.

After Apikalia's group went, it was the THEA SISTERS' turn. Colette, Nicky, Pam, Paulina, and Violet had been practicing for months with the help of their DANCE instructor, Professor Plié. Their **hard work** paid off — by the time they finished, the five mouselets were tired but proud.

At the end of the morning, Apikalia's team was in **fiRSt PLaCe**, followed by the Thea Sisters, and then the Ruby Crew.

Colette, Nicky, Pam, Paulina, and Violet quickly changed out of their *costumes*. They were about to exit through the stadium **GATES** when some rodents from the Maui team approached them. The team's captain was the **YOUNG** Hawaiian rat Nicky had

noticed the night before.

The ratling **_gazed_** at Nicky as he said hello. Then he asked, "Do you like **SURfinG**?"

SURF'S UP!

Nicky was struck squeakless, so Pam JUMPED right in. "I'm sorry, but is that a question or an invitation? And could you tell us your name again? We didn't quite CATCH it."

The ratlet BURST out laughing. "My name is Renani, and it was an invitation. Surfing on the first afternoon of the competition is kind of a TRADITION. Everyone gets to know one another a little better, and we get to relax and catch a few waves. Would you like to join us?"

"Of course!" answered

Nicky ENTHUSIASTICALLY.

"But . . . don't we need to start investigating for Professor Van Kraken?" Paulina murmured.

"I have an idea! Let's mix business with PLEASURE. If we go surfing, we'll get to check out the beach," said Pam.

"Oh, all right," Paulina relented. "We'll hit the surf. But keep your eyes open, okay?"

Nicky gave her a quick hug. "You know we will, Paulina!"

Pam grinned. "Cowabunga, dude!"

An hour later, the Thea Sisters found themselves down at the *beach*. It was packed with young mice. All the HULA competitors were there, and they were all surfing!

The Ruby Crew was part of the crowd. The mouselets were scampering across the sand

and showing off their surfboards.

Nicky immediately jumped into the water with Renani. When Ruby spotted Nicky's **WiLD** surfing moves, it gave her a sneaky idea!

"Nicky is really reckless," she told her friends. "And surfing is a **DANGEROUS** sport. What if she had an accident? Then it'd be good-bye hula competition for the Thea Sisters!"

PAMELA

coLette

NiCKY

PauLiNa

VioLet

Alicia, Connie, and Zoe immediately caught her drift. They leaped into the **WATER** on their surfboards. Ruby wanted to surround Nicky and push her into the *waves* to make her lose her balance.

But Ruby and her friends severely underestimated Nicky's surfing skills. She was practically an **EXPERT**. She darted away easily, and Ruby and her friends found themselves on a collision **COURSE** — with one another! They all ended up underwater as a **GIANT** wave washed over them!

"Uh-oh!" cried Renani. "Those mice **wiped out**! I better give them a paw." He **HURRiED** over to help the Ruby Crew. Without him, the mouselets would have been cast adrift for a good long while.

THE LEGEND OF THE FIRE FLOWERS

Nicky returned to the beach with her surfboard under her paw. Her friends were smiling as they ran to meet her.

"Great job!" said Pam, giving her a high five. "You were really shredding waves out there! I don't know what Ruby was up to, but Renani was nice enough to take her and her buddies to the infirmary."

But Nicky wasn't paying attention — she'd just noticed that someone was watching them. "Look! It's the old gentlemouse we saw yesterday!" she exclaimed. "The one who said the hotel was DANGEROUS. . . ."

"Let's go talk to him while he's here!" added Paulina.

Just as they were about to reach the elderly mouse, someone else **marched** up to him. It was **Ekana**.

"You need to stop **disturbing** the resort guests with your nonsense!" he said to the mouse, shaking his paw. "This is the last time I'm going to warn you, Grandpa Nahele!"

Paulina *jumped*. "What? This is your *grandfather*?"

But the two mice were too busy **ARGUING** to hear her.

"Ekana!" said Nahele fiercely. "You know I'm not making up **NONSENSE**! I'm telling you the truth! Why won't you listen?"

Ekana **LOOKED** ashamed.

Nahele took advantage of his silence. "The resort was built in a very **DANGEROUS** location. Now you dare to ignore the signs that **Nature** is giving you just because you want to make a quick buck?!"

Ekana crossed his paws skeptically. "What signs, Grandfather?"

"The appearance of the WHITE DOG in the city is one," Nahele responded.

Ekana rolled his eyes. "Oh, yes, that's scientific proof for you!" Then he changed his TONE. "All you're doing is **discrediting** my business. The news hasn't reported any danger of an **eruption**, and neither has the research observatory. So leave my guests alone!"

With that, Ekana turned tail and **stomped** off.

Nahele looked after him sadly. Then, finally, he noticed the Thea Sisters. "My grandson is a good, honest rodent," he told them. "The problems started when he let that **sewer rat** Sammy Sharkfur convince him to build the resort. I don't like Sammy. He is very powerful, and I'm afraid his business is shadier than it seems. . . ."

Paulina helped the elderly **gentlemouse** sit down. "Can you tell us about the white dog?" she asked. "What does that have to do with Mauna Loa erupting?"

"The white dog is part of an ancient Hawaiian legend — the Legend of the Fire Flowers," explained Nahele. "It says that every time a white dog appears in the city, the volcano will **SHOOT OUT** fire flowers. In

other words, there will be an eruption." The elderly mouse suddenly stood up. **"LOOK!"**

The mouselets followed his **GAZE** and saw . . . the WHITE DOG! The animal stopped for a moment, looked over, then loped away.

The Thea Sisters EXCHANGED a look of determination. Legend or not, the moment had arrived for them to do some serious investigating!

EVERYTHING'S UP TO CODE!

Colette, Nicky, Pam, Paulina, and Violet *hastily* returned to the resort. They wanted to ask around about Sammy Sharkfur.

First, the mouselets went to the reception desk and explained that they were doing some **RESEARCH** for an in-depth article about the resort.

"Is it possible to see the surveyor's report on this **area**?" asked Paulina. "We were told that an accurate survey of the land was done. . . ."

"**EXTREMELY accurate!**" confirmed the young rodent at the reception desk, showing them a pile of documents filled with data and graphs. "The construction is up to code. There is absolutely **ZERO** danger!"

It looked like she was right. Judging from the row of STAMPS on the lower part of each document, everything was official and aboveboard.

Next the mouselets wandered around the resort and approached staff members to ask what they thought of Sammy. But everyone

had nothing but **praise**.

Not only that, the idea of Mauna Loa erupting made everyone the Thea Sisters interviewed *smile*. After all, if it wasn't in the news, why should they **worry**?

The mouselets didn't give up. They decided to continue their search for information in **HILO**, the city nearest the resort.

"Let's start with the closest news bureau," Violet said. "Everyone keeps mentioning the news, saying no one has reported any risk of **ERUPTION**. So maybe a local **newspaper** office can tell us something!"

FiRST STOP: THE LOCAL PAPER!

The five mouselets headed for Hilo, planning to contact the *editor* at one of the local newspapers. They bought several papers and settled onto a park **BENCH** to figure out where to start.

Colette, Nicky, Pam, Paulina, and Violet paused to enjoy the view of the Hawaiian **sunset**: It was truly **gorgeous**! Then they decided which paper to visit first and climbed into a taxi that *darted* through the streets of the city. It left them in front of the office of the most famouse local newspaper.

The mouselets scurried inside and introduced themselves as **young** journalists. They were greeted by Melika, the paper's editorial director.

"Have you heard anything recently about possible *activity* from Mauna Loa?" asked Colette.

Melika **shook** her snout. "No. At least,

not in the last few years. You see, Mauna Loa hasn't erupted since 1984."

Paulina was puzzled: It really seemed like no one had any reason to **worry** about an eruption.

Just as the Thea Sisters were about to **LEAVE**, Melika said, "If you want to learn more, you could go straight to the **SOURCE**."

The **mouseLets** didn't understand, so Melika explained, "You should visit the research observatory. That's where we get all our information about the **volcano's** activity."

THE PLOT
THiCKEnS. . . .

The Thea Sisters said good-bye to Melika and **HURRIED** out of the office.

"So," murmured Violet thoughtfully as they took the **ELEVATOR** down, "if there's something SUSPiCiOUS going on, we'll find the data at the observatory, right? That seems to be where all the news about the VOLCANO comes from."

"That's definitely where we need to go!" Paulina replied.

Outside the building, the mouselets were looking for a TAXI when they noticed a police car parked nearby. It seemed to be **waiting** for them. Leaning against the doors were the two **POLICE OFFICERS** who had asked Nahele to leave when the mouselets

CLUE!

had first arrived at the resort.

The two officers **WATCHED** them for a moment. Finally, one squeaked, "Aren't you here for the **HULA** competition? Isn't it a bit late to be out and about?"

The other one nodded. "He's right. It would probably be best if you were **safe** and sound back at the resort."

It's the two police officers again! Their behavior seems more suspicious than ever. . . .

73

THE PLOT THICKENS. . . .

The Thea Sisters looked at one another in surprise: That sounded more like a **THREAT** than a piece of friendly advice!

Violet squeezed Paulina and Pam's paws. "They're right," she agreed loudly. "*Let's go*, mouselets!"

As they were **LEAVING**, she whispered to her friends, "I think it's better to not attract attention from those two. I have a sneaking suspicion they aren't **POLICE OFFICERS** at all!"

"Yeah," Pam whispered back. "The fact that they took the trouble to come all the way here looking for us just confirms something fishy is going on."

Colette, Nicky, Pam, Paulina, and Violet returned to the resort. As they were passing through the lobby, they noticed **Sammy Sharkfur** squeaking on his cell phone.

Quiet as mice, the Thea Sisters hid behind

an **ENORMOUSE** plant and started eavesdropping on his conversation.

"No, they haven't come back yet, but I want you to keep an **EYE** on them from now on, understand?! Those five rodents are **NOSIER** than an aardvark at an anthill! They are asking too many **QUESTIONS** around

here, and I don't like it."

The mouselets looked at one another in SURPRISE. Was Sammy Sharkfur talking about them?!

Sammy concluded the conversation with an angry gesture. Then he strode down the hallway that led to the Thea Sisters' suite.

"He was *obviously* talking about us!" declared Colette as soon as they were sure they were alone.

"We need to be very CAREFUL from now on," said Pam.

"Agreed," said Nicky, yawning. "Now let's hit the hay. We have a busy day tomorrow. Just thinking about dancing the modern choreography contest is making me stress more than Santa Paws on Christmouse Eve!"

The plot thickens! Why did the two police officers (if they really are police officers) follow the Thea Sisters? And what is Sammy Sharkfur hiding?

PSSST... PSSST...

The next day was dedicated to all of the individual performances and the group performances with **modern** choreography. For this stage of the competition, Colette had outdone herself. She had **DESIGNED** eye-catching costumes with a gorgeous **red-and-white** floral design.

The Thea Sisters were **WORRIED** about wrinkling their delicate costumes on the bus ride, so they decided to bring them to the stadium and get changed there. They dressed in their usual clothes and carefully **folded** Colette's designs inside their backpacks.

"Everyone ready?" Nicky asked. Her friends nodded. "Then let's roll!"

The five mouselets *scurried* downstairs

to meet the other contestants in the lobby. They joined Apikalia's group and began chatting away.

Zoe noticed the Thea Sisters at once. She **ELBOWED** Ruby to get her attention.

"Pssst . . . pssst . . ." she whispered.

"What is it?!" snapped Ruby, adjusting her dress with one paw.

Zoe pointed to the Thea Sisters. "Look, they have their costumes in their backpacks."

Ruby glanced over at the THEA SISTERS. Then she looked back at Zoe as if she were mold on a cheese slice. She was getting more and more **IRRITATED**. "So? Do you really have to update me on their every move?" she answered RUDELY.

Zoe shook her snout and leaned in close to her FRIEND'S ear. "Well, imagine what would happen if one of them were to LOSE

her backpack. All five mouselets would probably have to back out of the competition! Then it'd be bye-bye second place, *aloha* first place for us!"

Finally, Ruby understood what Zoe was getting at. An unpleasant *smile* spread across her snout. "Zoe! Have I ever told you that I absolutely *adore* it when you're *smarter* than I am?"

Zoe smiled, too. Her plan was a go!

TOTAL CAT-ASTROPHE!

The bus arrived RiGHT ON TiMe.
Nicky found a seat next to Renani, and they
immediately started TALKING about
the previous afternoon's surfing. The drive
passed quickly.

At the stadium, the stage had been adorned

with hundreds of orchids. Everyone *oohed* and **AAHED** over the gorgeous flowers.

As she was admiring the **DECORATIONS**, Colette felt someone bump into her. She almost lost her balance and had to stumble to stay on her paws. She assumed it was an accident till she felt a *tug* on her back.

Colette *whirled* around in surprise. Behind her stood Alicia, who was blushing **bright** red. "S-so sorry, Colette! Someone pushed me!" she mumbled.

ZOE'S PLAN

Alicia pretends to bump into Colette . . .

. . . and steals her costume out of her backpack!

Colette was squeakless for a second, but then she smiled **kindly**. "No worries, it was just an accident."

Alicia turned to Zoe, and the two *ran off* together.

Ruby and Connie were waiting for them. They **GIGGLED** as they watched their friends approach.

"Did you get it?" Ruby whispered.

"Of course! It was easier than taking cheese from a mouseling. I put it in my bag," Zoe replied **triumphantly**.

Alicia passes the costume to Zoe . . .

. . . and then apologizes to Colette, who doesn't notice a thing!

The other mouselets high-fived her.

"I just **wish** I could see the look on their snouts when they realize it's gone!" snickered Alicia.

In the meantime, Colette had returned to her friends without **suspecting** anything was amiss. The individual competitions had begun, so the Thea Sisters hurried into the changing rooms to **DRESS** for their performance.

As soon as she opened her backpack,

Colette let out a cheese-curdling shriek. "**AHHHHH!**"

"Good Gouda, Colette, you're going to give me a **heart attack**!" said Pamela. "What in the name of cheddar is going on?"

But Colette didn't answer. She was busy thinking, retracing her steps, trying to figure out when it could have happened. Suddenly, she **exploded**, "What a down and dirty **TRICK**!"

"What? What did you say?" asked Nicky.

Colette showed them her pink backpack: It was **EMPTY**! "I was tricked! Alicia bumped into me — at first I thought it was just an accident, but now I'm pretty sure she did it on purpose so she could **steal** my costume! Without it, we can't participate in the competition!"

The mouselets were as **frozen** as fish sticks.

"You mean . . . your costume is **gone**?" asked Paulina in shock.

"This is a cat-astrophe!" cried Violet.

"This whole thing smells fishier than day-old tuna! We can't just do nothing and let them win!" spluttered Nicky. She turned and **scurried** out the door.

She was rushing down the corridor when she ran into Renani, whose eyes **sparkled** when he saw her. But he quickly turned serious when she exclaimed, "Renani, I need your help! We need to find Colette's costume right away — someone stole it!"

Renani was just as indignant about the **THEFT** as the Thea Sisters. "I know just what to do," he said **CONFIDENTLY**. "You and your friends go backstage and wait for your turn. I'll take care of the costume!" he **ASSURED** her.

Nicky scampered back to the changing room and told her friends Renani would help them. A few minutes later, as they were nervously waiting in the wings (there were only two groups before them!), Renani hurried over to join them. He had a satisfied expression on his snout. In his paws was Colette's **costume**!

Nicky hugged him. "How did you manage to find it?" she asked incredulously.

"**Simple!**" he replied with a wink. "I used the same STRATEGY they used to take it from Colette!"

Colette, Pam, Paulina, and Violet all clapped their paws.

"**Thank you**, Renani!" said Nicky. "You are a true pal!"

FULL SPEED AHEAD!

The recovery of Colette's costume gave the Thea Sisters an extra jolt of energy. They had a stellar performance and **JUMPED** to the head of the charts. Now they were even with Apikalia's team, whose good **SPORTSMANSHIP** put the Ruby Crew to shame.

"You were great! Compliments to Colette on her marvemouse costumes!" Apikalia congratulated them.

"**Thanks!**" Colette responded. Then she whispered to Violet, "We squeaked in by a whisker! Another moment and we'd have **missed** our chance to perform."

While everyone else returned to the hotel, the mouselets asked Renani if he'd accompany them to the observatory. Renani READILY accepted.

Nicky had told him their professor's suspicions about the VOLCANO, and Renani immediately offered to help the mouselets clear up the situation.

"We can go in my car," he suggested. "It's big enough to take us all, and it's the **fastest** way to get to the **NATIONAL PARK**. That's where the observatory is located."

The group scrambled into the **SUV**, and Renani got behind the wheel. The ratlet drove carefully, playing tour guide as they sped along. "The observatory was created to deal with the risks of the two **active** volcanoes in Hawaii: Kilauea and Mauna Loa. The park is actually a **NATURE** reserve —" Renani

HAWAII VOLCANOES NATIONAL PARK

Hawaii Volcanoes National Park covers a vast area on the island of Hawaii. The park extends from the sea all the way to the tops of Mauna Loa and Kilauea. Many protected animal and plant species live there — so many that the park was declared a World Heritage Site by UNESCO in 1987. The park also includes the Ka'u Desert, a region of unusual lava formations.

stopped abruptly and looked in his rearview mirror. "**UH-OH!** We've got company, mouselets!"

The Thea Sisters TURNED AROUND and saw a dark car *RACING* toward them. It looked like it wanted to run them off the road! Unfortunately, the car's windows were tinted, so they couldn't **SEE** who was driving.

"Something tells me that our fake-police friends are in that car," Violet said.

Nicky had an idea. She TURNED toward

Renani. "Do you think you can lose them?"

"Of course!" he answered, **GRINNING**. "I took a class in race-car driving! Actually, Nicky, I think you would've loved the class —"

Colette **coughed**. "Umm, fascinating as that sounds, I'm not sure this is the time to start comparing notes about MOUSCAR!"

Renani understood. He nodded and shifted the car into a *faster* gear. The **pursuers** tried to keep up. They gained ground on the SUV for a while, but Renani twisted the wheel this way and that, changing direction so suddenly that he was finally able to shake them.

"Yee-haw!" he cried, looking in his rearview mirror. There was no sign of the other car. "I think we did it! Let's take this little shortcut I know. They'll never look for us there."

The SUV bumped along a dirt road. After another minute, the mouselets SPOTTED the observatory.

THE OBSERVATORY

The Thea Sisters were **OUT OF BREATH** by the time the SUV pulled up to the observatory. Now that they were being tailed, the mouselets were really anxious to figure out what was going on. They needed to learn why the most **important** research center in the area had not gathered the same data as Professor Van Kraken and his team.

As they scurried into the observatory, the **mouseLets** were met by a group of young researchers. They seemed eager to help, but when Paulina asked them about the possibility of an **ERUPTION**, the researchers shook their snouts vehemently.

"**No way** is Mauna Loa about to erupt," one responded. "We monitor the activity for

Mauna Loa and Kilauea twenty-four hours a day. Our **instruments** are absolutely trustworthy. There hasn't been a single sign of an eruption. You really don't need to **worry**."

Yet the Thea Sisters didn't feel any better. They knew something wasn't **RIGHT** . . . but what?

"Ah, good morning, Professor!" exclaimed

one of the researchers **suddenly**. A tall, thin rodent had appeared in the doorway. The researcher turned to the mouselets. "Let me introduce to you the SCIENTIST in charge of the observatory, Professor George Crusterson."

The Thea Sisters **shook** the professor's paw. Then they said their good-byes. They had run out of questions.

As they were crossing the parking lot, it finally hit Violet. She slapped her snout. "Just a sec . . . **BY MY CHEESE**, I think I've got it!"

Do you recognize the head of the observatory? No? Well, then turn back to page 33 and take a look at the rodent talking to Sammy Sharkfur the night of the welcome party!

MOVE THOSE TAILS!

Renani looked at Violet quizzically. "What do you mean?" he asked. "The SCIENTISTS at the observatory all seemed very nice to me. Even their boss was nice!"

Violet shook her snout. "Their **boss** is the whole point! We *already saw* Professor Crusterson! He was talking to Sammy Sharkfur the other night, and he kept looking around **suspiciously**. Do you remember, mouselets?"

Her friends nodded in EXCITEMENT.

"So you think Professor Crusterson is helping Sharkfur **hide** something?" Renani asked.

"Until now, our SUSPICIONS were based only on Professor Van Kraken's data.

But we finally have something more — a connection!" Paulina exclaimed.

"**SO?** What do we do now?" asked Colette.

"Before we do anything, let's talk to Ekana," Violet suggested. "It's possible he doesn't have anything to do with this whole situation, but he may have other **important** information."

"Great idea," said Pam. "All right, then, what are we waiting for? Let's move those tails!"

The Thea Sisters and Renani jumped back into the **SUV** and headed to the resort. But they were in such a hurry, they didn't notice that someone was watching them. . . .

YOU'VE SEEN TOO MANY MOVIES!

Once they were back at the resort, the Thea Sisters said good-bye to Renani and **headed** straight for Ekana's office. Before entering, they made sure that Sammy Sharkfur was **nowhere** in sight.

Unfortunately, explaining their theory to Ekana was no EASY task. In fact, when he heard the mouselets' story, he started laughing.

"So, let me make sure I've got this straight," he said. "You're asking me to believe that Sammy and a famouse scientist are deliberately DECEIVING all the rodents on the island, including me? And that Sammy built the resort in a DANGEROUS spot, even though he knew that the volcano could wipe it out?! HA, HA, HA! Mouselets, you've seen too many disaster movies!"

Ekana got up from his desk and led the Thea Sisters to the door. "Now, if you'll excuse me, I have a lot to do today, and it's getting late," he declared.

But Paulina was determined to get him to listen. "What if we're right? What if your

grandfather is right, too? We're just trying to protect you from Sammy's shady business."

Ekana was caught **off guard**. He looked confused.

Nicky went a step further. "What if Mauna Loa **ERUPTS**? The fate of all the resort's guests is in your paws! Don't you think that it's worth investigating to see if there's any **truth** to our suspicions?"

Ekana weighed their words thoughtfully.

After a moment, he sighed and agreed. "Oh, all right. Tell me what you have in mind."

Violet smiled with relief. "Okay, now we're cooking with cheese! Tonight we'll return to the observatory and look for PROOF. If Professor Crusterson and Sammy Sharkfur are working together to COVER UP a possible eruption, we'll discover the truth!"

The Thea Sisters left Ekana's office feeling satisfied. But once again, they didn't realize someone was WATCHING them. . . .

THE HUNT FOR PROOF

Colette, Nicky, Pamela, Paulina, Violet, and Ekana waited for **dusk** to return to the observatory. Renani offered to drive them again in his SUV.

As the SUV bumped along the mountain trail, Ekana **shook** his snout and mumbled skeptically. "Mauna Loa about to erupt? What a load of **GOAT CHEESE** . . ."

A few minutes later, they pulled up to the entrance of the national **PARK**. Renani parked the SUV, and the group continued toward the observatory on paw.

Inside it was totally dark, except for the lights from the seismographs and the computers over where the **night** team was working.

SEISMOGRAPH

A seismograph is an instrument that is used to record details about earthquakes. The seismograph detects the ground's movement and represents it on a graph (seismogram) as a series of waves and peaks. Since volcanic eruptions can cause earthquakes, scientists use seismographs to monitor volcanic activity.

The group snuck into the room they'd visited that morning. Quiet as mice, they began to **rummage** around the desks and the files, searching for documents that might reveal the truth about the possible eruption.

Colette, Nicky, Pam, Paulina, Violet, Ekana, and Renani looked thoroughly. But there didn't seem to be anything unusual. Paulina examined the charts from the **seismographs**, but they all seemed normal, without any peaks that would indicate imminent **DANGER**.

"Everything seems to be in order here!" said Pam, **PUZZLED**. "We've got to be missing something. . . ."

"See? What did I tell you?" protested Ekana. "Let's go! We've already broken the law, coming in here without permission looking for who knows what!"

While Ekana and Pam argued, Paulina

THE HUNT FOR PROOF

ducked under the desks and began sifting through the WiReS that fed into the computers.

"Check this out!" she exclaimed. She pointed to a **BOARD** on the ground. Her friends huddled around to get a better **LOOK**.

"This explains why none of the researchers of the observatory have noticed anything **SUSPiCiOUS**!" exclaimed Paulina triumphantly.

"What explains it? I'm still lost," said Colette. "As far as I know, that *thing* could be a CD player, or even a fur dryer!"

Paulina laughed. "This is a digital selector — a device that gathers all the information from the seismographs and 'selects' which information will be sent to which computer."

Colette stared at her BLANKLY. So did Nicky, Pam, Violet, Ekana, and Renani.

"I'm afraid you're going to have to spell it out for us, Paulina," said Nicky. "It's like you're talking in **Feline** and we're all squeaking Rodentese."

"Let me just look at one thing, and then I can explain it more clearly," said Paulina, delving into the mess of cables and electrical leads.

SURPRISE!

After untangling a few wires, Paulina stood up and grinned with **SATISFACTION**. "Just as I suspected!" she exclaimed **TRIUMPHANTLY**. "The selector is linked to George Crusterson's computer!"

Everyone was hanging on her every word, especially Ekana, who watched her with a **worried** expression on his snout.

"Using this **device**, Crusterson is able to filter the information coming from the observatory's instruments through his computer," Paulina explained, disconnecting the selector. "He's been deciding what information about Mauna Loa's VOLCANIC activity passes through to the other computers!"

"That explains why the other researchers don't know about the possible eruption!" Nicky said. "Professor Crusterson STOPPED them from monitoring the volcano's actual activity! He filtered all the data coming in so they only saw what he wanted them to see!"

Ekana was squeakless.

Paulina **sketched** in the plot's details. "So it went like this," she guessed, **LOOKING** Ekana squarely in the eye. "Sammy Sharkfur **convinced** you to become his partner so he could build his resort and take advantage of your land's MAGNIFICENT view of the volcano."

"There was just one problem," continued Pam. "He had to *silence* any rumors about potential eruptions!"

"So Sammy bribed the head of the observatory, George Crusterson, to **hide** the data showing the VOLCANO'S activity," Colette put in.

"And as long as the observatory didn't pick up any volcanic activity, none of the newspapers would ever know about the **DANGER!**" concluded Violet.

Ekana was about to respond in disbelief when someone clicked on the **light** and started applauding.

clap clap clap

SEVEN WITNESSES TOO MANY

Sammy Sharkfur was standing in the doorway. He stared at the Thea Sisters, his **EYES** sparkling with sinister intention. Professor Crusterson and the two fake **POLICE OFFICERS** were next to him.

"Nice work, you little snoops!" he declared. "You really stuck your snouts into my business."

Ekana pointed a paw at him **threateningly**. "You . . . you . . . you wretched ratfink! You **fooled** me, and you tricked all of Hilo!"

Sammy brushed away Ekana's paw. "You are so **naïve** that it wasn't even fun fooling you!" he sneered.

Ekana darted toward him, but one of the

fake police officers 𝖻𝗅𝗈𝖼𝗄𝖾𝖽 him while the other grabbed his paws and pinned them behind his back.

"Don't waste your time attacking me, partner," Sammy said **mockingly**. "You see these two gentlemice? They work for me!"

"Of course they do!" Paulina said. "I'll bet they aren't even **real** police officers!"

"Another brilliant deduction, my dear mouselet," Sammy said. "You've really managed to **SURPRISE** me!"

"You have no idea how much information you can get by **POSING** as a police officer," said one of the thugs.

The thug who was holding Ekana let go and pushed him toward the mouselets. "Though I must admit that you were pretty sharp to spot us," he **SNAPPED**.

"Do you realize that you've put the entire population of Hilo in **DANGER**? How can you be so reckless?" demanded Paulina.

Sammy laughed **uproariously**. "Listen to this rodent! 'The entire population'! Why should I care about the population? I'm afraid this adventure is over now. From this moment on, you and your friends are just seven witnesses too many!"

The two thugs grabbed Nicky, who was closest to them.

"Get your paws off her, cheddarface!"

Renani **SHOUTED**, jumping forward.

Ekana **RUSHED** forward to give him a paw, but Sammy was quicker. He **TRIPPED** his partner, who stumbled toward the ratlet. They both **FELL** to the ground in a heap.

The two fake cops regained control of the situation. Within a few moments, the Thea Sisters, Ekana, and Renani were bound and **gagged**.

"Where should we put them, boss?" the first thug asked.

"Leave them in the basement," said Professor Crusterson. "No one ever goes down there, and if they **SCREAM**, the walls are soundproof."

"Good idea," said Sammy. He grinned at the Thea Sisters. "Your new accommodations won't be quite as **DELUXE** as the resort's!"

Professor Crusterson and his thugs led the

THEA SISTERS, Ekana, and Renani toward a SMALL door. The PRISONERS were forced to scurry downstairs into a windowless basement room. Once they were inside, the two fake police officers BOUND their feet along with their paws. Then they shut off the lights and slammed the door behind them.

DARKNESS enveloped the room. The Thea Sisters and their friends were trapped!

PRISONERS!

Colette, Nicky, Pamela, Paulina, Violet, Ekana, and Renani felt lost. They tried to wiggle and **WHIMPER**, but with their snouts shut tight, they couldn't communicate with one another. And they couldn't see anything about the room they were locked in. **ESCAPE** truly seemed impossible!

"If only I could get my paws free!" thought Nicky, **TUGGING** her paws and feet with as much force as she could muster. She tried dragging herself across the ground toward one of her friends, but all she did was knock herself against the walls and get bruises all over her tail.

"It's useless. We'll never be able to get out of here!" she thought, disheartened.

The others made similar escape attempts. But everyone soon realized that it was impossible. They were **bound** too tightly.

Just when they were losing all hope, they heard the **sound** of a latch opening. Suddenly, a ray of **light** shone through the dark room.

"Are you all right?" asked a husky voice. The Thea Sisters immediately recognized that squeak: It was Nahele! Ekana's grandfather had come to **SAVE THEM**!

Using his cane, Nahele slowly descended the stairs and began to untie the prisoners.

"I had a feeling Sammy Sharkfur was up to something, so I **waited** near the observatory. I saw you arrive first, and then him. The rest

you know," the old mouse explained.

The mouselets **sighed** in relief. It was ironic that no one had believed this **kind rodent**, yet he had been right all along!

As soon as Ekana was free, he stood up and gave Nahele a hug that was both *grateful* and apologetic.

"**GRANDFATHER**, you must forgive me. I should've listened to you. Sammy Sharkfur is nothing but a slimy sewer rat. I was too naïve — just a **RatLet** playing at being a businessmouse!"

Nahele shook his snout **UNDERSTANDINGLY**. "It's normal for you to want to find your way, Ekana," he said. "But sadly the world is full of rodents without CONSCIENCES. The important thing is to stand by your values and know when to admit your mistakes. And that's just what you are doing now!"

Once Ekana and Nahele had untied all their friends, the little group CLIMBED the stairs and peeked into the observatory's office.

An **unpleasant** surprise was

waiting for them: The lights of the seismographs were all flashing at once, and the instruments were going off crazily. This could only mean one thing. SEISMIC activity was occurring. Mauna Loa was about to erupt!

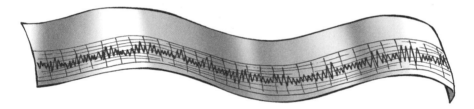

LAVA ALERT!

The Thea Sisters looked at one another in dismay. **SOMETHING** had to be done immediately, but what?

After a moment's confusion, Paulina snapped into action. She grabbed her phone and called Professor Van Kraken.

"Professor, you were right about everything!" she EXCLAIMED. "We're at the observatory, and the instruments are going crazy. Mauna Loa is going to erupt any minute now!"

The professor stayed calm. "It's okay, Paulina. Listen to me carefully. Based on my **calculations**, the lava will flow in the direction of the resort. You need to get over there right away and *evacuate* the building. Bring everyone to safety, do you hear me?"

"**Loud** and clear!" Pam chimed in.

The mouselets, Renani, Ekana, and Nahele ran to warn the researchers in charge of the **night** watch. Then they darted outside.

At that moment, there was an extremely **VIOLENT** rumble, followed by a sharp **shake** beneath their paws. Mauna Loa was about to explode!

There wasn't a minute to lose. Everyone jumped into Renani's **SUV**. They sped over to the resort faster than a mouse can smell melting cheese.

The guests and the hotel staff were all

sleeping, so no one had noticed that there was lava **flowing** toward the building.

The mouselets, Renani, Ekana, and Nahele **dashed** inside and began knocking on all the doors.

"Wake up! Mauna Loa is ERUPTING!"

"Everyone outside at once! You can't stay here, it's too dangerous!"

"Run away! Get to safety!"

"Quickly, there's no time to lose!"

The guests began to spill out of their rooms in FEAR.

Ruby opened the door to her room and began adding to the chaos. "Danger? What DANGER?! You're just being DRAMA queens as usual!"

THE USUAL DRAMA QUEENS

Ruby was determined to make the Thea Sisters look **bad** . . . even at a time like this! She stalked out of her room, shouting, "One little rumble, and you all start **yelling**! Don't make a mountain out of a mousehill. Just shut your snouts and — **HEY!**"

Colette had grabbed her by the paw and pulled her toward the window. Fiery sparks were **SHOOTING OUT** of the mouth of the volcano, and a flood of lava was sliding steadily toward the resort. It was growing bigger and faster the closer it came.

Ruby's eyes opened so wide they looked like they were about to **POP** out of her snout. She **BURST** into tears and hugged Colette tighter than a mousetrap spring. "Help! I'm begging you, don't leave me alone!"

Colette disentangled herself and tried to calm Ruby down. "Don't worry, if we can get everyone out of the hotel, no one will get hurt!"

Ruby dried her tears and began to knock on every door she saw. "Everyone out! The volcano has erupted, your lives are in danger!" She shouted so loudly that the guests who were still uncertain immediately *hurried* out.

Meanwhile, Ekana, Renani, and Nahele escorted the hotel's staff outside. Then they did a quick snout count to make sure no one was left in the building.

"Hurry, come this way!" ordered Ekana. "Everyone, get in your cars and drive toward the bay!"

It was a *RACE* against time: The

LAVA was picking up speed. It THREATENED to catch up with them any moment now.

As their SUV **sped** down the road, away from danger, Pam noticed a ray of **light** coming from a room high up in the resort. She could see the **shadows** of rodents moving around up there.

"Wait just a sec. **LOOK!**" she shouted. "There's still someone in there!"

Ekana followed her gaze. "That's the window of Sammy's office!"

YOU AGAIN?!

The SUV quickly retraced its route to the resort. The **THEA SISTERS** ran up to the office and burst in to find Sammy Sharkfur crouched in front of an open **safe**. Next to him were George Crusterson, who was *shining* a flashlight inside the safe, and the two fake officers, who were putting piles of **MONEY** inside a backpack.

Pam turned on the overhead light, which startled the four dirty rats so much they practically **jumped** out of their fur. "Surprise!"

"You again?!" said Sammy with a start. "But . . . how did you get **FREE**?"

"Pretty incredible, huh?" teased Nicky. "We're great detectives, *plus* we have more

LIVES than a whole pack of street cats!"

"Okay, that's it for the witty wisecracks," said Paulina, stepping forward. "Come on, we need to get out of here. The resort is about to be flooded with **LAVA**! If you stay here, you could be **KILLED**!"

"Nonsense!" replied George Crusterson. "According to my **calculations**, the lava will

never reach the resort. It's just a false alarm."

As if in response, a strong rumble **shook** the building, and a burst of light **illuminated** the room.

One of the fake officers ran to peer out the window. The lava had reached the wall surrounding the resort and was pressing closer and closer. The whole resort was surrounded by an eerie, glowing **light**.

"They're right!" the officer cried in **SURPRiSE**. "On your paws, everyone. We gotta get out of here!" He and his partner **IMMEDIATELY** raced out of the room.

Sammy shot George a withering look. "You and your calculations!" he thundered. "You're a dunce, that's what you are! Expert seismologist, my paw! You're nothing but a **QUACK**!"

The **THEA SiSTERS** exchanged a surprised

glance. "Takes one to know one, I guess," muttered Pam.

At that moment, a dense **WaVe** of lava began to envelop the resort. The mouselets didn't waste another second. They pushed Sammy and George out of the room and out into the resort's circular driveway.

In the rush to escape, Sammy **DROPPED** his backpack full of money. Just as he realized he had lost it . . . it was engulfed in lava! **WHOOSH!**

The Thea Sisters and the two **thugs** reached safety in the nick of time. An instant later, the resort was swept away by lava. The glowing red tide devoured everything in its path: buildings, rocks, trees — it was all **swallowed** up.

"M-my . . . my money . . ." Sammy Sharkfur moaned in dismay. But it was too late.

YOU GET WHAT'S COMING TO YOU

Sammy Sharkfur and George Crusterson had barely escaped with their fur. But a bitter surprise awaited them. The two good-for-nothings quickly realized that rescue teams of **firefighters** weren't the only ones greeting them — the real police were there, too. In fact, their two fake–police officer friends were already sitting inside a real police car — in **pawcuffs**!

"What is going on here?!" yelled Sammy.

The police commissioner took two more pairs of pawcuffs off his belt. "Sammy Sharkfur, we've had our eye on you and your **ACCOMPLICES** for a while now! We have evidence that proves you corrupted dozens of officials to get the permits for your resort's construction."

Sammy Sharkfur was sweating more than a SHINY slice of Swiss.

"That's not all!" the COMMISSIONER continued, getting angry. "You tricked your business partner into pawing over his land. You and George Crusterson HID information about Mauna Loa, risking the safety of the entire Hilo population. You and your accomplices are under arrest!"

After a moment, Sammy regained his usual confidence. "Under arrest?! With what proof?" he said scornfully. "You don't have any! My office has been swept away by LAVA! There are no documents; it's all lost! So there is NOTHING you can prove about me or my business."

"Oh, there's proof, all right!" interjected Paulina suddenly. She pulled out her **MousePhone**.

Sammy looked at her quizzically. Professor Crusterson turned PALER than a ball of mozzarella.

"You forgot about today's technology, Mr. Sharkfur," Paulina said **SHARPLY**. "My MousePhone is an **EXCELLENT** recording device!"

Paulina pressed a button, and suddenly

Sammy's squeak rang out loud and clear: "Why should I care about the population?" **Luckily**, Paulina had thought to hit RECORD on her phone in her pocket when Sammy and his friends discovered the THEA SISTERS at the observatory!

Paulina pressed the **STOP** button, and everyone turned toward Sammy Sharkfur.

Sammy's **ARROGANCE** had slipped away like cheese off a cracker, and he was left angrily **squeezing** his paws into fists. "I would've gotten away with it, too, if it weren't for you meddling mouselets!" he cried.

A NEW DAY

At **dawn** the next day, the volcano finally stopped erupting. The last of the lava **SLID** into the ocean without causing any further damage. Fortunately, the only building that was damaged was the Fire Flowers Resort. That wasn't too big a surprise: It was the only building in the path of the **VOLCANO**!

"It had to end this way," **sighed** Ekana, resigned.

The Thea Sisters, Renani, Ekana, and Nahele were at the shore, watching the **red-hot** lava slowly fade on the volcano. What an incredible spectacle of **nature**!

Nahele put a paw around his grandson. "You will soon find your **WAY**, grandson. And this time, no shortcuts!"

Ekana *smiled* at him. "I learned my lesson! I'm just glad no one was hurt." He turned to the **THEA SISTERS** and bowed. "I have you to thank for that."

Colette, Nicky, Pam, Paulina, and Violet blushed from the tips of their snouts to the

tips of their tails.

The little group began to walk toward the city stadium, where the HULA competition had been held. That's where everyone had agreed to meet after the eruption. Because of the state of **EMERGENCY**, the competition was suspended, and no winners were announced. It would be postponed until the following year.

Instead of BEING UPSET about the competition, Ruby thanked Colette and the other Thea Sisters. "I have to admit, if it weren't for you mouselets, I'd be a roasted rat right now!" But she couldn't resist adding, **"Obviously**, the Ruby Crew already has next year's competition all sewn up!"

ALOHA OE!

It was time to go home. All the hula competitors headed over to Hilo airport to catch their planes and say good-bye. Everyone had managed to save a bit of LUGGAGE from the volcano. Even the Thea Sisters each had a small backpack. In fact, Colette had **somehow** managed to save her pink purse, her rolling suitcase, and her COSMETICS bag.

"Colette, I can't believe it! How were you able to take all of that stuff during the **chaos** of the eruption?" **exclaimed** Nicky.

"This was the bare minimum for me!" Colette explained, **shrugging**.

Renani offered to drive his new **friends** to the airport. When it was time to say good-bye, he and Nicky **HUGGED** warmly.

"Here, I got something for you," said Renani shyly, pulling a small package from his pocket.

The mouselet **UNWRAPPED** it eagerly. It was a CD of Hawaiian songs! "Just a little something to **remember** me by," Renani said.

Nicky smiled and **BLUSHED**. "Thank you! I

can't wait to listen to it."

"Nicky? I don't want to **INTERRUPT**, but our plane is taking off any minute now," said Pam.

So the mouselets said their good-byes. As soon as the *plane* took off, Nicky started

listening to the CD. It was filled with **Beautiful HAWAIIAN** songs about friendship. She curled up in her chair and let herself be swept away by the music. She sighed *happily*. Soon, she'd dozed off with the headphones still on her ears, and the music *warmed* her heart all the way back to **WHALE ISLAND**.

ANOTHER GREAT SCOOP

When the Thea Sisters got to the end of their **TALE**, I was **spilling over** with questions. "So, what happened to Sammy Sharkfur, Professor Crusterson, and their accomplices?" I asked, curious.

"They're in the 𝕊𝕃𝔸𝕄𝕄𝔼ℝ, where they belong!" Pam responded.

"They got what they deserved, all right!" agreed Colette.

"Once the police started investigating Sammy Sharkfur, they discovered other **shady** deals he'd made," Violet explained. "He had a habit of **TRiCKiNG** locals and creating businesses that only helped himself, just like the one with Ekana."

"**HOLEY CHEESE**, mouselets! What a great scoop! This story has it all," I exclaimed. "Ancient legend, ***mystery***, adventure and, most important, true friendship!"

THEY WERE MORE THAN FRIENDS. THEY WERE SISTERS!

Thea Sisters

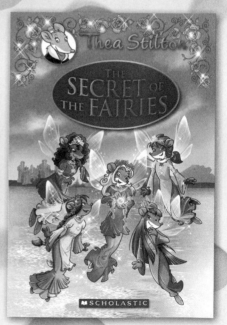

Check out these very special editions featuring me and the Thea Sisters!

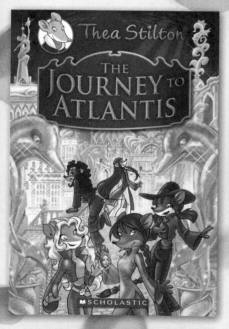

THE JOURNEY TO
ATLANTIS

THE SECRET OF
THE FAIRIES

Don't miss any of my fabumouse adventures!

Thea Stilton and the Dragon's Code

Thea Stilton and the Mountain of Fire

Thea Stilton and the Ghost of the Shipwreck

Thea Stilton and the Secret City

Thea Stilton and the Mystery in Paris

Thea Stilton and the Cherry Blossom Adventure

Thea Stilton and the Star Castaways

Thea Stilton: Big Trouble in the Big Apple

Thea Stilton and the Ice Treasure

Thea Stilton and the Secret of the Old Castle

Thea Stilton and the Blue Scarab Hunt

Thea Stilton and the Prince's Emerald

Thea Stilton and the Mystery on the Orient Express

Thea Stilton and the Dancing Shadows

Thea Stilton and the Legend of the Fire Flowers

Want to read my next adventure?
I can't wait to tell you all about it!

GET INTO GEAR, STILTON!

I was selected by the mayor to give a special driving demonstration, but my driver's license had expired! I had only a week to relearn everything to pass the test for a new one. Little did I know that that my lessons would introduce me to a talking robot car! It was up to us to stop a thief and make the roads safer for everyone.

Be sure to read these stories, too!

#1 Lost Treasure of the Emerald Eye

#2 The Curse of the Cheese Pyramid

#3 Cat and Mouse in a Haunted House

#4 I'm Too Fond of My Fur!

#5 Four Mice Deep in the Jungle

#6 Paws Off, Cheddarface!

#7 Red Pizzas for a Blue Count

#8 Attack of the Bandit Cats

#9 A Fabumouse Vacation for Geronimo

#10 All Because of a Cup of Coffee

#11 It's Halloween, You 'Fraidy Mouse!

#12 Merry Christmas, Geronimo!

#13 The Phantom of the Subway

#14 The Temple of the Ruby of Fire

#15 The Mona Mousa Code

#16 A Cheese-Colored Camper

#17 Watch Your Whiskers, Stilton!

#18 Shipwreck on the Pirate Islands

#19 My Name Is
Stilton, Geronimo
Stilton

#20 Surf's Up,
Geronimo!

#21 The Wild,
Wild West

#22 The Secret
of Cacklefur
Castle

A Christmas Tale

#23 Valentine's
Day Disaster

#24 Field Trip to
Niagara Falls

#25 The Search
for Sunken
Treasure

#26 The Mummy
with No Name

#27 The
Christmas Toy
Factory

#28 Wedding
Crasher

#29 Down and
Out Down Under

#30 The Mouse
Island Marathon

#31 The
Mysterious
Cheese Thief

Christmas
Catastrophe

#32 Valley of the
Giant Skeletons

#33 Geronimo
and the Gold
Medal Mystery

#34 Geronimo
Stilton, Secret
Agent

#35 A Very Merry
Christmas

#36 Geronimo's
Valentine

#37 The Race
Across America

#38 A Fabumouse
School Adventure

#39 Singing
Sensation

#40 The Karate
Mouse

#41 Mighty
Mount
Kilimanjaro

#42 The Peculiar
Pumpkin Thief

#43 I'm Not a
Supermouse!

#44 The Giant
Diamond Robbery

#45 Save the
White Whale!

#46 The Haunted
Castle

#47 Run for the
Hills, Geronimo!

#48 The Mystery
in Venice

#49 The Way of
the Samurai

#50 This Hotel
Is Haunted!

#51 The Enormouse
Pearl Heist

#52 Mouse in
Space!

#53 Rumble in
the Jungle

#54 Get into Gear
Stilton

Don't miss these very special editions!

THE KINGDOM OF FANTASY

THE QUEST FOR PARADISE:
THE RETURN TO THE KINGDOM OF FANTASY

THE AMAZING VOYAGE:
THE THIRD ADVENTURE IN THE KINGDOM OF FANTASY

THE DRAGON PROPHECY:
THE FOURTH ADVENTURE IN THE KINGDOM OF FANTASY

THE VOLCANO OF FIRE:
THE FIFTH ADVENTURE IN THE KINGDOM OF FANTASY

Meet
GERONIMO STILTONOOT

He is a cavemouse — Geronimo Stilton's ancient ancestor! He runs the stone newspaper in the prehistoric village of Old Mouse City. From dealing with dinosaurs to dodging meteorites, his life in the Stone Age is full of adventure!

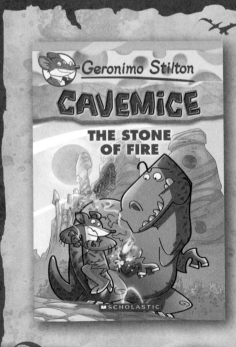

Geronimo Stilton
CAVEMICE
THE STONE OF FIRE
SCHOLASTIC

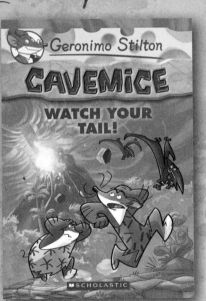

Geronimo Stilton
CAVEMICE
WATCH YOUR TAIL!
SCHOLASTIC

Meet
CREEPELLA VON CACKLEFUR

I, *Geronimo Stilton*, have a lot of mouse friends, but none as **spooky** as my friend CREEPELLA VON CACKLEFUR! She is an enchanting and MYSTERIOUS mouse with a pet bat named **Bitewing**. YIKES! I'm a real 'fraidy mouse, but even I think CREEPELLA and her family are AWFULLY fascinating. I can't wait for you to read all about CREEPELLA in these fa-mouse-ly funny and **spectacularly spooky** tales!

#1 THE THIRTEEN GHOSTS

#2 MEET ME IN HORRORWOOD

#3 GHOST PIRATE TREASURE

#4 RETURN OF THE VAMPIRE

#5 FRIGHT NIGHT

THANKS FOR READING,
AND GOOD-BYE UNTIL OUR
NEXT ADVENTURE!